Our beautiful planet is dying.
It needs help if it is going to survive.

This help comes in the form of a group of
children who have been given some magic
powers.  This is their adventure.

**Let's hope they are successful!!**

This is their story described by
DAVID WRIGHT

To Isabelle
I hope you enjoy this
Love from
David x

# Contents

written & illustrated by

DAVID WRIGHT

## Arin and Elik devise a plan

Arin and Elik are two of the guardians of the universe

with specific responsibilty for the Earth.

They communicate through 'thoughts.'

Arin sent a thought to Elik 'I'm worried the Earth is dying.

Its ecosystems are being destroyed.

Animal and plant species are becoming extinct and the

atmosphere is warming up and becoming toxic.'

'Yes' agreed Arin, 'but this has happened many times

before on the Earth.  It has always lived on the edge,

lurching from one crisis to another.

Yet it always survives.'

'Yes maybe so' thought Elik, 'but on top of all this is the most recent problem of a serious viral pandemic.'

'I see what you mean' thought Arin, 'this is creating many more serious issues which could be the final tipping point.
Let's face it, the live on guardians, the HUMANS, have some very big challenges ahead!'

'As do we of course' thought Elik, 'We have to help by showing them the error of their ways. If they are to survive both crises, we need to get them to RETHINK.'

'BEAUTIFUL isn't it?' they both thought.

'We must save it!'

So Elik and Arin put their heads together

to try and work out how to make this happen.

Together they think.

'It is a difficult task, but the challenge is clear. They need to

show the humans what they are doing so badly and persuade

them to change, to work with the planet with nature to use

the resources more wisely and in a renewable way.

Only by doing this will the Earth have a future.'

Elik and Arin think long and hard.

'Who can they get to help? Too many of the leaders of the

World have failed. Whether due to greed, self interest, the desire

for power or just plain ignorance. So we cannot confidently use

them to help now. Who can we rely on to deliver the message?'

Elik suddenly has an inspirational thought

'Of course - let's use the most innocent, least polluted minds,

the CHILDREN.

After all, *IT IS THEIR FUTURE*

and they are the ones who will ultimately

have to live with the changes.'

Arin then had a brilliant thought 'Let's use our **magic children**, the ones we gave some magic powers to.' Elik soaks this thought up and is excited. They have the beginnings of a plan forming........

Elik and Arin are excited and want to get started.

'So let's think about the problems.

Why is the Earth dying?

What have the Human guardians got so wrong?'

Their thoughts merge.

'The problem is they haven't planned for the massive

**_population increase_**.

The Earth is getting close to the maximum it can support.

And all these people need **_somewhere to live_** so

more land has to be found.

They also need to obtain or produce **_more food_** which

means greater harvesting of other living organisms

or again finding more land for growing foods.

And lastly they will use **_more resources_** especially

**_energy_**. Of course there will be **_more waste_** to deal

with and all the consequences of this.'

### Edward and Eleanor visit the Amazon Rain Forest

Elik and Arin decide to use the children to tackle some of these problems by sending them to the areas where they are happening and finding out how bad the problems are. If they can speak to the people who are doing them they may be able to persuade them to stop or at least think more about their actions.

Edward and Eleanor slide down magic rainbows which mysteriously appear in the corner of a room.  But they had not had an adventure recently and had started to believe their magic rainbow had disappeared for ever. But tonight it had reappeared. They couldn't believe their luck and jumped on it as  quickly as they could.

To start with Edward and Eleanor had no idea where
the rainbow was taking them. But it was a long rainbow and as
they were sliding, Elik and Arin beamed thoughts into their
heads, strange thoughts about something called *deforestation*
- people chopping down trees to create space for growing food,
grazing animals and harvesting wood to make furniture,
houses and paper.

As they slid off the rainbow, they suddenly knew why they were
there and what they had to do.

Edward and Eleanor looked around. All they could see were men using electric saws to chop beautiful trees down and putting them onto lorries. They knew they had to do something to stop this.

Eleanor walked up to two men who had just completed chopping down a tree and started to talk to them, well almost shouted at them. Edward shook his head and joined her. He rarely saw Eleanor looking so serious. What was she going to say? Eleanor said lo the men "Why are you chopping down so many trees?" Edward had never heard her speak with such feeling and authority.

Eleanor didn't even give the men chance to answer but went straight into emptying her mind of all the points Elik and Arin had beamed in whilst she was on the rainbow.

"Do you know just how much good trees do for us? Do you realise that they are one of the main things that affect our climate, the temperature, how much rain we get and even the amount of wind. Trees are also the home for thousands of different animals from insects to gorillas. Many of the plants that live in forests provide medicines for diseases like cancer and arthritis."

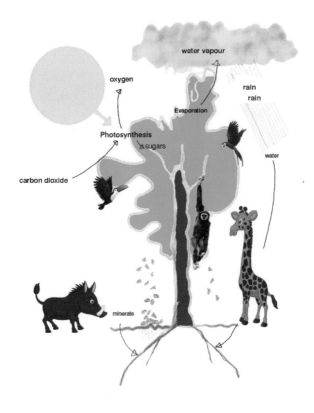

The men looked bemused, but she continued. "And what happens to the wood?" she asked. Before they could answer she continued. "Yes I do know we do need wood for building and to produce paper, and even some fuel, but not so much that we have to chop down **so** many trees. We also do not need the land it frees up. There is so much land on the earth we could use instead. And on top of that, If we burn the wood, it produces pollution, especially carbon dioxide."

The men protested and together said "It's just a job to us. We can't afford to think about this." Before they could say anymore, Edward said "OK time for some facts.

Currently forests cover 30% of the earths land, but if you keep chopping them down at this rate, 15 billion per year, in 100 years there will be none left.  Just think with no trees what will the quality of the air be like?  Did you know that 20% of the oxygen in our air comes from the trees in the amazon rain forest, the very trees that you are chopping down.  Carbon dioxide levels will rise causing global warming.  The amount of rainfall will decrease with no trees to recycle it and large parts of the earth will become desert.

More than 28000 animal and plant types will become extinct in the next 25 years because they will have no where to live and less food. I could go on......" Both Edward and Eleanor were  amazed at the knowledge they both seemed to have, but decided they had said enough.

The two men now had their heads in their hands and were staring at each other. "What are we doing?" one of them said. "We have to stop doing this" the other one said. They put their saws down and turned to the children and said "Thank you for telling us all this. We will never chop another tree down and will do our best to persuade the others to stop." They then shakily walked away towards some more loggers.

As the men walked away a rainbow suddenly appeared and Edward said to Eleanor "Come on this is our lift home." They ran to it and jumped on and before they knew it they were back home.

Edward and Eleanor could not stop thinking about the adventure
they had just had.  It had been very different to all their others,
but they hoped that this was just the start of many more.
They had talked to men who had the ability to make lasting
changes to help the earth recover and they wanted to do more.
They knew thay couldn't tell anybody about this, but would wait
for the next rainbow and the next part of the story..

Arin and Elik were also very happy. The first part of their plan
seemed to be working.

# Mikey swims with a dolphin

Mikey was playing on the beach when he saw a dolphin stranded at the waters edge. He ran to it and was shocked to see that it had a large piece of sticky plastic covering up its blow hole. The poor thing could not breathe and would die if not helped. Mikey quickly pulled off the plastic and then dragged the dolphin back into the sea.

Before it started to swim away, the dolphin said to Mikey, "Thank you for saving me. Would you like to swim with me?"

Mikey couldn't believe his ears - did this dolphin just speak to him? "Yes please" he almost shouted. Mikey was used to animals talking to him, but it still came as a shock.The dolphin said "OK let's go" and swam out to sea. Mikey started to follow but was worried about how far he could go. The dolphin said "Just follow me and don't worry, I'll look after you."

Suddenly the dolphin dived under the water and Mikey followed. He could breathe under water! He followed the dolphin, swimming alongside it and was not worried at all. They eventually came to a coral reef where the dolphin stopped. The dolphin said "Would you like to meet some of my friends?" Mikey said "Yes please." He somehow knew what he had to do next.

Mikey stood near the coral reef which he thought looked a little pale, not at all like the glossy photos he had seen. The dolphin said "These are some of my friends." There was a large crab, an octopus, an anglerfish, a lobster, a large clam, a seahorse and a giant turtle. They all said "Hello Mikey, it is nice to meet you." Mikey was amazed - they could all talk and knew his name, as if they were expecting him!

Mikey said "Hello, it is so nice to meet you all. I have so many questions to ask you." Elik and Arin had already beamed lots of thoughts into his head. He did not know this of course, but he did have this urge to ask lots of questions.

Mikey first turned to the coral and asked "Why are you looking so pale?" The coral animals amazingly could talk and said "It is because the green and red algae which normally live with us and supply us with energy and nutrients have left. They have been damaged by the warmer water temperature. I don't know how we are going to manage without them."

Mikey was shocked, but turned to the other animals and said "How has the the sea water getting warmer affected you?" The first to answer was the anglerfish. "It is getting more difficult to breathe as warm water holds less oxygen. This means I can not swim as fast as I did and do not feel safe from my predators." The seahorse said "The higher temperature also makes my young seahorses grow too quickly affecting their chances of surviving."

Before Mikey could say anything, the clam shouted out "Many of us are also being affected by the water being too acidic due to pollution caused by you humans. Many of us have have shells made from calcium carbonate and the acid is destroying this." The crab, turtle, and lobster all nodded and together said "Yes this is getting really bad." The coral added "Yes yet another problem for us as well, as if we didn't have enough already!"

Mikey was shocked, but also wanted to ask about waste being dumped into the sea. He was there, after all because of plastic waste. He asked "How is plastic waste affecting your ocean world?" The dolphin decided to answer this. "We are finding more and more of this. I really like humans, but you are dreadful at clearing up after yourselves. It is not just plastic of course, there are lots of different waste products, but plastic is the worse.

The plastic gets stuck in the gills of fish, stopping them from breathing and blocks the guts and feeding tubes of animals stopping them digesting their food. Too many animals are dying because of human waste." The turtle said "And we often see dead birds in the sea. The plastics get into these when they eat food. You humans have a lot to answer for!"

Mikey could go on forever, but he decided not to push his luck.

After all his body was not used to spending so long underwater.

He knew he had not asked about lots of issues he had in his brain,

but he said goodbye and asked the dolphin to take him back home.

The dolphin started to take him back to the beach. On the way Mikey

saw a lot of examples of what they had talked about - plastic waste

everywhere, pale coloured coral reefs and even a dead seagull.

Even the water felt too warm! He then saw a fishing net being

pulled along by a fishing boat. An Idea entered his mind and he

turned to the dolphin and said "Please take me back to your friends."

By the time he had got there, the plan in his head was clear.

Mikey told all the animals and they were all eager to get started.

Mikey knew that there was a problem with overfishing the ocean.

He decided to use the fishing net he had seen to send two

messages.

The idea was to help any fish caught in the net to escape and to

replace them with plastic waste. When the fishermen pull the net in

they will be shocked.  One by the amount of plastic waste and two

by the lack of fish. Messages delivered.

The octopus took control of this and managed to free the fish.

He then helped the crab, lobster, angler fish, seahorse and the

turtle to collect plastic waste and place it in the net.

After the dolphin had taken Mikey back to the beach, Mikey still felt very angry and upset. He knew he had delivered a message to the fishermen, but was this enough? He wanted to do more so he did some research and found out about the United Nations

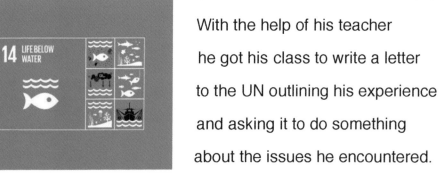

Global Goal 14 - Life Below the Water With the help of his teacher he got his class to write a letter to the UN outlining his experience and asking it to do something about the issues he encountered.

Mikey also had the idea of getting his scout group to do a beach clean. He told his school teacher about this and before long everyone in the school was involved in beach cleaning. During the cleaning Mikey also met up with his friends from past adventures, Larry the ladybird, the Lazy Bee and Mr.Frog and they agreed to help spread the message to their friends.

Elik and Arin were very very happy.

## Zac and Clive find some pollution

Things were going well so far, but there was still much to do. Elik and Arin decided to involve Zac next. They seeded his mind whilst he was asleep in bed. When he woke up, he couldn't stop thinking about air pollution and global warming. By chance he had arranged to meet up with his friendly cloud Clive and go for a ride and a chat as he hadn't seen him for a long time.

After breakfast Zac went out into his garden and Clive the cloud appeared. Zac was so happy and climbed onto him.

They took off on their planned adventure. Clive decided to follow the motorway as it was the quickest way to get to where they were going. Suddenly Clive started coughing. Zac was worried for his friend and asked him what was wrong.

Clive said "I have been coughing quite a lot recently. I think it must be all the air pollution." Zac said "That's strange as I was dreaming about air pollution last night. Let's change our plan and go look for some of this air pollution." Clive said "I can use my magic cloud dust to show it. Any pollution will turn dark yellow. We can start by looking at the pollution coming from the cars on the motorway below."

Clive moved down closer to the cars on the road below and sprinkled some of his magic cloud dust. Suddenly the exhaust fumes from the cars and the air around them all turned dark yellow. Goodness knows what the drivers thought about this!

As it got worse, the cars started to stop and the drivers got
out and started discussing where the yellow gas had
come from. Soon they realised it was pollution from their cars.
Zac and Clive looked down on this and thought good, if only
one driver stops driving because of this, it is a result.
Zac seemed to know all about the gases and said  "That is a
nasty mixture of gases."  He even knew some of the the names.

"I believe they are called carbon monoxide and carbon dioxide,
Carbon monoxide is a poisonous gas and carbon dioxide is what
we call a greenhouse gas. It absorbs heat and is helping to raise
the earths surface temperature, a process called global warming."
Clive was amazed by his knowledge and said so.
Zac replied "I told you that I was dreaming about this all night!"

Arin and Elik shared a nice thought. 'Zac is good'

Clive said "Let's find some more pollution" and moved higher before heading Inland towards some clouds. As they got closer they realised it was actually smoke coming out of a power station.. They eventually stopped over the towers and Clive sprinkled some cloud dust. Immediately the smoke turned dark yellow.

Again Zac seemed to know why and said to Clive "It is yellow because it contains some more of the nasty gases. There is some carbon dioxide, but also another very bad greenhouse gas called methane. There is also a gas called sulphur dioxide. Sulphur dioxide dissolves in rain to form acid which is then called acid rain. Acid rain kills trees, especially christmas trees, makes soil less good for growing food crops and kills many animals in lakes, rivers and oceans." "Thank you" said Clive, "you certainly are an encyclopeadia of knowledge."

The sky around the towers became filled with dark yellow clouds.

The workers came out of buildings to see what was happening

and stood there scratching their heads, trying to work out why.

The next day the local newspaper would contain pictures of the

yellow clouds and suggest it was due to pollution. It even linked it to

the yellow clouds on the motorway.

Arin and Elik couldn't be more pleased.

Both Zac and Clive were very quiet as they started heading for home.

Seeing so much pollution had shocked them. As they flew over the

fields, Zac said to Clive "I dont want to worry you any more, but my

dream also included cows in fields." Clive said "Dont tell me these

are creating pollution as well?" "I'm afraid so" replied Zac,

"cows produce a lot of methane, especially when they burp. Methane is a very serious greenhouse gas." Clive said "Maybe we should stop eating so much meat and drinking so much milk?"

Clive finally delivered Zac back home and said "I'm so sorry. This was the least enjoyable outing we have ever had. Maybe next time we can do something better." Zac said "Yes well maybe my dream happened for a reason. I hope your cough gets better." Zac went into his house and decided to write a letter to the UN in support of Global Action Goals 7 and 13. He would tell them about his experiences today. They wouldn't believe him of course, but...

He also felt a song coming on.

Zac's song

*Chorus*

*Tiny steps on tiny feet*

*Tiny acts help us to meet*

*Clean air targets for our world*

*Watch your dreams as they're unfurled*


See your targets hit the skies

See the people start to cry

Now at last we understand

just how precious is our land


So never think that you're too small

To start a change that's good for all

You really can protect our earth

make everyone see just what it's worth


*Tiny steps on tiny feet*

*Tiny acts help us to meet*

*Clean air targets for our world*

*Watch your dreams as they're unfurled*


Zac knew the very person to give this to.

# Beth and Izzy visit the Arctic

Arin and Elik were very pleased with their work. Using these children had been inspirational! Next they decided to use the magic skills of Izzy and Beth. Izzy and Beth have recently developed an interest in watching TV programmes about global warming. They have also been dreaming about it.

One sunny February day, Izzy said to Beth, "Why don't we go to the arctic and see for ourselves what is happening there?" Beth was happy to agree, but wondered how they would get there? She then remembered the magic shed and its rocket capsule. "Yes why not" she said, "we can use the rocket in the magic shed, if we can find it."

"Don't worry" said Izzy, "Edward will tell us where it is."

Before long they are sitting in the chair in the rocket capsule and telling it where to take them. A few minutes later the door opened and they stepped out into a winter wonderland. But there was a problem. They were on a piece of floating ice someway from the main ice mass. "No problem" said Beth, "I'll use my magic to freeze the water to form a bridge." They walked across this to the main ice mass. All around them were masses of seals, some walruses and even a pack of arctic foxes.

The girls had a good look around and everything seemed good
until suddenly a large piece of ice broke free and started drifting
away. "Well I never" said Beth, "there is a polar bear and its cub
on the lump of ice and it is looking a bit worried. Should we rescue
it?" Izzy said "No it is OK, I can read its mind you know."

But then the polar bear started growling. Izzy knew something
else must be upsetting it, so she focussed again on reading its mind.
The bear was very distressed about the loss of yet more ice.
The bear was worried about where it was going to catch its food
and raise its cubs if all the ice vanished. Izzy told Beth and
she asked "Can you read the minds of all animals?" Izzy replied
"Yes and all humans as well."

Izzy went in amongst the seals and walruses and started to read their

minds. The seals of course were not too unhappy as they knew it

would be harder for the bears and arctic foxes to catch them.

But they were worried about the decline in the number of fish in the

sea and for some reason they preferred the sea to be cold.

The girls knew from watching the TV programmes that the sea was

getting warmer because of global warming and warm sea meant

less fish. The  walruses and foxes were as worried as the

bears for the same reasons. Izzy shared this with Beth who said.

"Let's see what is happening in some other places." They

started to wander away from the waters edge and headed inland.

Soon they reached some huts with a few people walking around.

As they approached the huts, the people were amazed.  One said "What are you two young girls doing here?"  Beth said "We have come to see if everything we have seen on the TV is actually happening here."  The man said  "Well we are a research group looking at climate change and have been monitoring the arctic for many years now.  Believe me there have been many changes. The air and water have got warmer, the ice has been melting and the winters have got shorter. There are less animals and those remaining are finding it harder to survive."

Izzy asked  "Why?" "Global warming" said the man.

"Now would you like  something  to eat and drink?"

Before they left Beth asked "What happens to the water when the ice melts and how long before it has all gone?" The man said "The sea level rises are causing lots of problems in the sea and for the rest of the world. At the present rate of ice melting it will have all gone in 100 years and many coastal towns and cities will be under water." The man looked sad, but said no more.

Izzy took the opportunity to read his mind. It wasn't good news Yes he was worried about the animals, but also about the weather changes around the world, the storm surges, the flooding and the forest fires. She said to him "Don't worry, Beth and I are going to make sure all the children of the World know about this."

He looked bemused, but smiled.

Izzy and Beth made their way back to the capsule they came in, but hit a problem. There was a hungry polar bear following them and Izzy was frightened.

Beth took charge and turned to face the bear. She then pointed at it and it started to freeze, just enough to slow it down, but not harm it.

Then out of the sky came a flying unicorn.  The girls jumped onto it and before long they were back at the rocket capsule.

They thanked the unicorn and climbed into the capsule. The next thing they knew was that they were back in the magic shed. As they walked home, they formed a plan.

The first thing they intended to do was to contact their cousin Dexter and discuss with him how to raise awareness of climate change issues.  Dexter is a wizard with everything musical and at organising events.

### Dexter pulls it all together

Although Elik and Arin were super happy about what these children had achieved, they felt it would help if the message got to even more children.  So they also decided to enlist the organisational skills of Dexter.  Dexter is Mikey's brother and cousin to Zac, Edward, Izzy and Beth.  His particular skill is his ability to bring people together using music.  He is also able to get people to be kind and helpful to each other.

Zac had already contacted him and passed on the words of his climate song.  It needed music so Dex enlisted the help of his brother Mikey who is good at this. All three of them eventually had a tune.

Dexter then got his animal band together to play this and  Zac recorded it.

Mikey then had the idea of putting it onto his YouTube channel. You don't get many animal bands on YouTube so he felt it would get some attention. Indeed it did and within days went viral.

Even Elik and Arin were amazed.

Elik and Arin beamed thoughts about the UN 'Be the Change Event" to Dex. Dex checked this out on the UN website and decided to do it.

He summoned the rest of the children to a meeting and told them his idea. Each of them put in their own ideas based on their recent experiences.

Edward and Eleanor outlined their trip to the amazon rain forest and the message they would like to pass on.

**Stop chopping down trees and replace those already removed**

Mikey told them about his swim with the dolphin and the issues raised.

**Stop polluting rivers, lakes and oceans with acid rain, heat and wastes, especially plastics**

Zac outlined his cloud adventure and his hopes for the future.

· **Use cleaner energy sources and stop polluting the air.**

Beth and Izzy talked about the problems global warming is creating for the animals in the arctic and the worries of the research scientist.

**Reduce global warming to stop the ice melting and the climate disasters**

"Wow" said Dexter. "You have all been busy. Surely we can put something together to spread the message to more children, and even some adults." So they agreed on a date to have an event. They also all agreed that the main focus this time should be on **global warming** and **climate change**. Other issues can follow later. Now all they needed to do was to decide where and how. Dexter thought to himself 'We can use my animal band on YouTube to advertise it. This should get people to attend.'

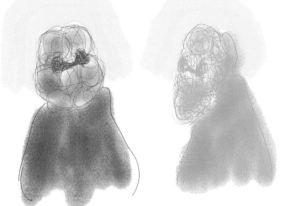

Elik and Arin glowed with delight.

**Covid brings HOPE**

Elik and Arin are happy about the way this has progressed and are sure it will steam roller into something big and have life changing effects, especially amongst the younger humans. There are lots more ecological issues to tackle and these children will help with these in the future.

But now they have to tackle the other big problem facing the earth, the Covid virus.

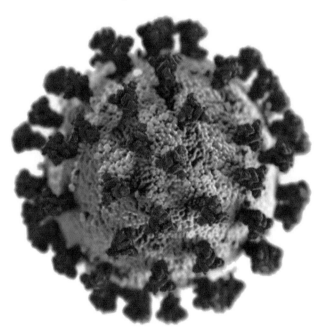

They know this is a big problem, but also that the humans have a good record of dealing with these. Arin thinks 'Yes but If only they would learn from past events, it would be much easier.'

They share each others thoughts, but all of a sudden Elik's dominate.

'Actually this virus has done us some good. If you think about it,
it has given the humans a glimpse of how it can be if they **act
now.** Covid has shown the way forward.' Elik's thoughts are
absorbed by Arin:

'Air pollution is much lower because less cars are on the road.
There is less air traffic and much of the large polluting industry has
temporarily stopped. Noise levels are down and you can hear loud,
happy birds singing. Animals are entering areas they have never
been to before and even the humans are reconnecting with and
appreciating the beauty of nature. They are even being kind to
each other and helping people they do not even know. In short, the
Earth has become a better place.' Arin had to agree.

'Covid has given the humans a view of what it could and should
be like. **There is HOPE, the Earth can have a future.'**

## Acknowledgements:

Original concept by David Wright

Written and illustrated by David Wright

Addditional illustrations supplied courtesy of Freepik.com
& Shutterstock.com

A very big thank you to Ann Carlin for allowing me to use her
Magic Children characters and for her editorial advice

Amazon-kdp.amazon.com

## Research sources:

Sir David Attenborough's magnificent catalogue of documentaries about
Life on Our Planet

www.worldwildlife.org/

www.un.org/

National Geographic magazine

Printed in Great Britain
by Amazon